THE PUPPETEER OF OBJECTS
A LYRICAL POEM

KATHLEEN M. JACOBS

Jan-Carol
Publishing, Inc
"every story needs a book"

The Puppeteer of Objects:
A Lyrical Poem
Kathleen M. Jacobs

First Edition Published October 2018
Little Creek Books
Imprint of Jan-Carol Publishing, Inc.
Cover Design: Anna Hartman

ISBN: 978-1-945619-75-5

You may contact the publisher:
Jan-Carol Publishing, Inc.
PO Box 701
Johnson City, TN 37605
publisher@jancarolpublishing.com
jancarolpublishing.com

For Anna Hartman
Student, Teacher, Friend, & Colleague

Also by Kathleen M. Jacobs

Honeysuckle Holiday

Marble Town

Collected Curiosities:
Poems, Essays, & Opinions

Please Close It!

THE PUPPETEER
OF OBJECTS

Puppeteer: a person who manipulates an inanimate object

that might be shaped like a human, animal or mythical creature,

or another object to create the illusion that the puppet is "alive."

ACKNOWLEDGMENTS

Continued gratitude—always—to Anna Hartman for donning so many creative hats throughout the process of writing this work. And always, too, to my husband, John, for more than I can possibly list in an acknowledgment—your unquenchable thirst for a good read and your ability to spot one that isn't— thank you, thank you.

PREFACE

Whether they observe from a tabletop or peek out from an opened drawer, objects that have been acquired over a lifetime become faithful friends, mute friends keeping safe life experiences, secrets, treasured moments, reminders of unpleasantries not to be repeated, or pleasantries to try to replicate, knowing full well that they will most probably not materialize — to return is an illusion in itself. These objects remain constant, no matter what life tosses our way. And yet, these inanimate objects take on a near-embryonic state, growing into "aliveness," as they invite us to see them for much more than what they appear. And then we too evolve, by their gentle nudge, into much more than we appear. After the gestation period, we each reach fruition and wonder at our earlier resistance to maturation.

Objects evoke emotion, memories. They invite us to not only look at them — *really* look at them — for what they truly are, but also to wonder at what they see in us when they look back, as if their respective senses are as acute as ours. We are changed by them in ways that surprise us, even after numerous observations. And in wondering what they might see in us, rather than what we might see in them, opens up a whole new world of possibilities — for each of these treasured objects embraces us as much as we embrace them. And in the observation, what might emerge is a discovery in ourselves that catches us completely unaware. And too, we are challenged to meld with these inanimate objects in ways that are both familiar and foreign. It's a bit paradoxical, isn't it? And it's in that paradox that we step gently into the adventure, not certain where one foot placed in front of the other might lead us but never for an instant

1

hesitating to take that first step, for it is in our nature to be curious where the journey will lead.

So let the journey begin with the call to board a vessel that assures us the journey might bring a blossoming over time, with no masked pretensions, as refreshment waits and stories unfold. And with the needle wavering in all directions, knowing that each one holds something fresh to experience while a sweet sing-song greets us at most every turn, we pull from a weathered envelope words that once and may still hold us captive. Blurred images come into clear focus, and we listen to the sounds found inside a seemingly hollow shell that we were once so certain resonated with us; now the shell is questioned, as we choose first one and then another adornment that fits who we once were, who we are now, and who we one day hope to be.

TRAINS

"All aboard!"

And with that certain invitation, each of the five senses comes alive. We find that most alluring, until the plush aubergine velvet interior seats beckon with equal enthusiasm in a sound that is as soft as a whisper as the engine roars and gathers momentum, making its way along a solid, seemingly interminable track of steel through the flat farmlands of the Midwest; the raw, western desert landscape; the snow-capped mountains of the northwest; and the soulful Blues of the deep south. Its sleek, polished exterior sets the stage for a beguiling landscape of transparency, if we don't make the mistake of denying the revelation of its promise to be more than we appear — to embrace all that we are and all that we could be. Not fully knowing where the prairie ends and the sky begins sets us on a course of true, intrinsic personal discovery.

And then there's the intoxicating allure of Grand Central Terminal in the city that never sleeps, with the magnificent, gently-detailed mural painted on its vaulted celestial ceiling. The design of the constellations, the starry representations, adds to the historic allure of this treasured edifice. And with little fanfare, Orion and Taurus keep company on the painted cerulean ceiling with the fish, the scales, the rams, and the crabs as each either contrasts with or complements the other, living harmoniously among the stars. And like the meandering locomotive's hurried passengers, it is often overlooked, yet insistent on halting those who resist.

3

The white linen-covered tables in the dining car are reminders of luxurious travel when Brooke Trout was introduced by the martini's second cousin, the Gibson, the pickled cocktail onion replacing the briny olive. And if we close our eyes very gently, we'll find ourselves traveling alongside Cary Grant and Eva Marie-Saint as the 20th Century Limited weaves its way ever so meticulously from New York City to Chicago. And our eyes remain closed for much longer than they should.

In their haste, they're not looking: not feeling, not tasting, not smelling, not even hearing a single morsel of what surrounds them. It is a pity. For in missing the velvety touch of a plush aubergine seat or tasting — actually tasting — the Brooke Trout or its precursor decorated cocktail, they can't possibly feel the excitement of the journey, the anticipation of the arrival, the intoxicating conversation with a complete, yet perhaps equally-intoxicating passenger headed (or not) to their destination, but to a destination that promises (or not) a yet-undisclosed treasure. They deprive themselves of the feel of a turned-down bed or the tip of a porter's hat — yes, that still happens with train travel. And as the train makes its way along its course, the trees and the snow-capped mountains; the arid, unadorned but shimmering desert; and the sweet notes upon arrival in New Orleans are missed. And by the time they're recalled, it's much too late.

TAUT STRINGS BIND AND TIE,
UNTIL THE PUPPETEER DIES.

ORCHIDS

The melding of colors, the fragility of the blossoms, and the sturdiness of its branches are met with an approachment of delicacy that suggests uncertainty. Yet we move towards it with certain trepidation, a bit off-balance until upon closer examination we are assured that trepidation was completely unnecessary. And the orchids, like the Munchkins, chuckle at our ignorance.

The stages of its blossoming are not unlike our own maturation. In reproduction, for instance, the orchid is versatile, but selective. At times, in adapting themselves to a variety of pollinators, they may or may not seek consent. For instance, the Ophrys apifera—better known as the bee orchid, a moniker that is so much more approachable—attempts to mimic the insect in order to attract a pollinator. Well. The flower looks like a receptive female, and the bee finds itself caught in its nest. The unknowing insect, in seeking the flower's nectar, is caught unawares in its slippery, tight pouch. Darwin wrote about both.

We somewhat become one with the orchid. Its fragility is childlike, innocent, delicate, and minimal, yet we're wary. Like a child, its complexity is subtle. Its velvety blossoms, hypnotic. Its layered detailing, at times, barely discernable. We find ourselves searching for a magnifying glass that will reveal all its hidden intricacies, intricacies that we so closely guard. And yet, it urges us to explore its myriad layers, peeling back each one to discover yet another. It's cyclical. It taunts and teases. And we're drawn in, like an elixir that takes its time to manifest itself deep within us.

With over 35,000 different species in existence, it seems as if nothing can impede their growth. They thrive on trees, rocks, in and under the ground, and in high mountain or bog locations. They even welcome the ants to help ward off enemies. The ants.

Ah, yes, we're rather cunning, without letting on — or at least without intense effort. Like you, we wait, even though time is of the essence. We are fully aware that we have limited time — anywhere from three to twelve weeks (perhaps slightly longer) — to tempt with our seductive color, fragrance, allure, and inherent tactile tendencies. We're patient, until we're not. In our short blossoming lifespan, we waste no time; there is no time to waste. Life is fleeting, and the cost of gambling a single moment is unfathomable, for it's the moments that count. We know it, and deep down, so do you. And it doesn't become universal until our blossoms lay scattered along the polished tabletops or huddled at the soil's surface. But by then, it is too late.

TAUT STRINGS BIND AND TIE,
UNTIL THE PUPPETEER DIES.

WATCH FACES

"The trouble is you think you have time."

– Buddha

The never-ending circle, the bold-faced numbers, the straight-up stroke of midnight or noon, the movement of the hands, and the measured reminder of the certainty that time is ticking away. The tick-tock sound seems to increase in intensity, until we are reminded of Edgar Allan Poe's "The Tell-Tale Heart." Until, if we're not careful, we too begin to entertain the anxiety that passing time delivers.

It was our bespectacled founding father who coined this phrase with such brilliance: "Do not squander time, for that is the stuff life is made of." And so, without much effort on our part and yet fully aware of our actions, we hold the watch face to our eyes and to our ears, most times believing that what it reports is more real than what we want it to read.

The urgency and immediacy of each telling, each reporting of what was missed — what has passed without fanfare — becomes disturbing, because we did not treasure its simple gift of wonder. "It can't be!" we proclaim incredulously. "It simply can't be! How did that much time escape? What did I do with it?" we ask, as if more than mere seconds, minutes, or hours have passed without our knowledge, as if time itself is to blame.

The recording of time from birth to death is imminent. Historically, a mourner would stop the movement of the clock to record the precise time of death, and we frighteningly yearn for the power to do just that, stop the clock. But that is not something that us mere mortals can ever attain, and that realization brings with it tremendous consternation. And we're often surprised by our own unwilling acceptance.

Learning to tell time — for most of us on the face of a cartoon character wristwatch — was a welcomed novelty. It was somewhat like learning to ride a bicycle or drive a car, until we fell into its incessant ticking; by then it was too late. We couldn't turn back the hands of time, no matter how much we sought to do just that. We came to know it, and that's when we knew of its importance and value, until we indeed began to squander it: to turn against that wise, bespectacled founding father. It had us in its grasp, and we held on to it while at the same time wanting to release its firm hold on us.

Their gaze is intense as they look directly at me, their eyes squinting as if blinded by the sun. And they look often, as if I may have stopped or at best simply missed a beat. They know time is running out, and they find this realization incredulous, time and time again. They always find it incredulous. They yearn to control it, but they have relinquished their control of it to the universe. They grimace at my passing, certain that what I reveal is not accurate. They find themselves checking other watch faces: their cell phone, the dash of their car, their wristwatch, the center of a train terminal, the courthouse square, only to discover that once again, they have lost another minute, or two, or three, or . . . They are dismayed, yet they continue their hurried pursuits, not having learned much of anything. And I, in my calculated certainty, have no other way of reminding them that I will continue to move along, much like them, save for the realization that I instinctively know that I'm going to keep ticking away, until the imminent point in time where I am stopped. It will not be by my own doing, but caused by a force much greater than myself, a force that will still the hurried. Regardless of my certainty, they will not cease to believe otherwise.

TAUT STRINGS BIND AND TIE,
UNTIL THE PUPPETEER DIES.

MASKS

Long before we can adjust the snap of the elastic cord around the back of our heads without assistance, we welcome and become accustomed to the transformative allure of masks: to their disturbing yet inviting comfort, to be whomever we choose to be, simply by wishing it so. The immediate attachment to the textured surface (be it paper, cloth, fiber, leather, painted or not, embellished or plain) masks in mere seconds all imperfections, much like a brightly-colored floral wallpaper covers damaged plaster or drywall. And we foolishly convince ourselves that the imperfections are, indeed, hidden.

Masks represent supernatural beings, fanciful or imagined figures. They've been worn for sacred purposes and in ancient rituals, worn to frighten, amuse, deceive. They are disguises to cover what secretly yearns to be revealed, that which no longer enjoys the frightening, dark corners of denial. But the self-imposed, all-too-familiar trappings are much too agreeable, their hold nearly impenetrable.

The childhood attraction to wearing masks of cartoon characters, princes and princesses, and animal figures can segue into festivals—Halloween, Mardi Gras, or any variety of masked balls—until they are shelved and stored, their disguises no longer needed. These disguises are as plentiful as the stars in the sky, and as mysterious; only the wearer knows the depths and deceptions of its mystery. And still, there aren't enough stars in the sky to cover every foible.

After thousands of years in use, their extinction is not a threat. And we revel, with tears in our eyes, at that realization, embracing it with a fierce gentleness.

Masks: tangible objects keeping watch — or so we think — over countless, intangible truths.

The Bard professes, "All the world's a stage, and all the men and women merely players." Ahh, 'tis true, 'tis true. And yet, we wear the masks as if we foolishly, yet knowingly misinterpreted Paul Laurence Dunbar's clear, concise admonishment. But never fear, I will assist until you no longer need my assistance. I will guard and protect until you are capable of embracing that responsibility. I know, it will take time. I will not leave you in the dark until the light becomes your true compass. But together, we can relinquish your hold and insistence on my guard over your pretensions, fears, and uncertainties. "Come out, come out, wherever you are," holds nothing but the promise of transparency.

So let's together link arms, knowing, ". . . if our gospel be hid, it is hid to them that are lost . . ." (II Corinthians 4:3).

TAUT STRINGS BIND AND TIE,
UNTIL THE PUPPETEER DIES.

BAR CARTS

It isn't just the cut-glass and crystal decanters that lure with their amber bourbon, clear vodka and gin, light and dark rum, and orange liqueur, the sun pouring in and ricocheting off the polished brass cart, sending rays of light in all corners of the room (particularly the dark ones), but also the aroma of fresh citrus and simple syrup, maraschino and Amarena or bourbon cherries. It's also the clinking sounds of garnish picks and shakers and jiggers, bar spoons and paring knives, citrus juicers, and tumblers, coupes, and Collins glasses. It's dizzying, and that was its intention from the start: keeping us off-balance, in more ways than one.

And then there's the list of classic starter drinks: Old Fashioned, Luis Buñuel Dry Martini, Daiquiri, and Gin and Juice Swizzles.

And certainly, the background music reels it all in, a cacophony of sounds nearly as essential as the well-stocked traveling bar cart. Think Rat Pack (Sinatra, Martin, Davis, Bishop, and Lawford). Think Las Vegas casino scene. Think Los Angeles home of Humphrey Bogart and Lauren Bacall. Think "You're

Nobody Till Somebody Loves You," "Theme from New York, New York," "My Way," "Strangers in the Night," "That Old Black Magic," "The Impossible Dream." And suddenly, it's all possible.

Visualize the fashions: sharkskin suits, slim ties, fitted dress shirts. Think "Mad Men" and "The Help:" tailored sheath dresses, fit and flare dresses with boat and sweetheart necklines, controlled curls and strands of pearls.

All of it, a mingling of the mind and the spirit, with the complete acceptance of what the melding will bring individually and compositely, regardless of the price. And like a fine theatrical stage set, the start button is pressed, and someone shouts, "Action!" And the magic continues until someone shouts, "Cut!" and "That's a wrap!"

The clink of brittle ice in an old-fashioned, swirling through the amber liquid; the sultry sounds from the LP spinning slowly on the record player; the click-click of a woman's heels on the polished wood floor; the smoke rings melding one to the other; and the innocuous – or not – winks suggesting more than idle chit-chat crescendo until, until tremors more than quiver and everything and everyone appears to defy gravity, while the pull is irresistible.

TAUT STRINGS BIND AND TIE,
UNTIL THE PUPPETEER DIES.

BOOKS

Lined up on a shelf, stacked in a corner (every corner) of a room (every room). Illuminated by our own imaginations, by the single bulb of a table lamp, or a ray of sunlight streaming in through an open window. Stories that will illuminate our thoughts, our beliefs, our creativity, our sense of the world around us. Characters that become more than personas we've discovered on a page in a book. Books evolve into friends we take with us to lunch, to the theatre, tucked securely beside us, as we drift off to lands unknown, waking in the middle of the night to open them with ease, picking up where we left off as if nothing much happened in between. As if they are all there is or needs to be.

Beginning with the delectable intrigue of Grimms' and imitating the rhythmic allure of Seuss, we cautiously ventured into the wild things that Sendak created, which fueled the beginnings of our own wild imaginations. And having tasted the morsels of those early worlds, we picked up our speed as we devoured Carle and Potter, Dahl and Milne, holding tight to not only the melodious nuances of the words, but also to the charm and comfort of creatures we came to know all too well. And Margaret Wise Brown put us to sleep every single night.

As we took steps to challenge not only our thoughts but our imaginings, it was L'Engle and Lewis, DiCamillo and Allsburg who set us on a course which would forever ignite our wonderings. And Gaiman and Patterson, Henkes and Selznick, and countless others would gently nudge us into lands unknown, promising enrichment and delivering every single time.

And as we moved along this road of discovery, challenge, and understanding we encountered entirely new worlds that we didn't even know awaited, yet we so hoped did. Works like *To Kill a Mockingbird, The Great Gatsby, In Cold Blood, The Handmaid's Tale, Native Son, An American Tragedy,* and *The Heart is a Lonely Hunter* became our compasses to explore unknown, uncharted, waters. And we gladly met the pull every single time, knowing that we could never — nor did we want to — extinguish the flame that kept burning and burning, igniting in us the quest for more — always the quest for more.

And as our thirst continued the constant need to be replenished, we were carried to yet another shore that offered a refreshment unlike any we had ever experienced before. Yet it was one that so seamlessly melded with the others that they all seemed to merge into one continuous, never-ending, somehow satiating progression of a completely insatiable appetite for more — always more. And that's what cummings, Dickinson, Frost, Plath, Whitman, Hughes, Hall, Kenyon, and Oliver brought to the feast.

It is perhaps books that will bridge and bind, challenge and ultimately bring together those alike and different to understand and accept the myriad worlds and peoples, ideologies and beliefs, possibilities and certainties that twenty-six letters of the alphabet — tossed like a handful of jacks, meeting one another as if in a whispered interlude to come together — after mixing and matching in innumerable ways to form words that anger and move, change and covet, incite and comfort, much like — or perhaps even more so — the humans who pen them that will become the ultimate gift. And it's the intoxicating and addictive aroma of ink on paper, whether leather-bound or hand-stitched, that will lure everyone to slide from the shelf a story that either very much defines who they are, or encourages them to discover a side of themselves that even they, in all their ignorance, had yet to make acquaintance.

TAUT STRINGS BIND AND TIE,
UNTIL THE PUPPETEER DIES.

COMPASSES

Even in our attempts to steady the circular apparatus, with its quivering magnetic needle and points printed on a circular rotating bezel, the needle floats on liquid so it can rotate freely; the red end always pointing to magnetic north. Unfailing precision at its core, with a luminous strip to assist in navigation at night and a magnifier for detailed map reading. It would seem that all the i's have been dotted and the t's have been crossed; there appears to be no room for error. And yet, its very purpose is to direct: to assure us that we are on the right path, despite our uncertainty.

Our physical journeys point us in all directions—north, south, east, and west. But perhaps it is equally important that the figurative direction our lives take follows much the same course: weaving and detouring, considering alternate routes, at times putting down roots and staying for a while. And yet, much like the needle of a compass, our journeys are seldom steady, always wavering—until they're not. Perhaps, at first, we might sense that ease of unwavering steadiness. But eventually, for most of us, those moments of a sense of settlement begin to quiver just a bit, and we as vehicles of constant change find ourselves shifting to a new direction, perspective, or understanding of the world around us — or, perhaps more importantly, of ourselves.

Set against the backdrop of an often unsteady-center, we wonder and wander about like a flock of geese thinking we're headed in one direction, surprised to find that the journey ends at a most unplanned, yet promising spot on a map, intentional destination or not.

When early sailors used the compass to ensure their course, it would have been unfathomable to any of them that its certainty could ever be doubted. And yet, each of us doubts their infinite certainty; how absurd, how incredulous, how offensive, how very contrary to their proven record.

Their hands tremble as they attempt unmercifully to keep level the needle's movement, uncertain where they want to arrive — whether or not they even want to leave — believing firmly in their own ridiculous notion of control. The movement is unnerving at times, for they are insistent on questioning its validity as their ignorance seeps deeper. And it is not until they relinquish their overly-firm hold that they can even begin to let it do the task for which it was destined to do.

TAUT STRINGS BIND AND TIE,
UNTIL THE PUPPETEER DIES.

BIRD NESTS

The combination of mud, twigs, leaves, and feathers is collected and often formed into a cup-shaped vessel, one that is hidden — as much as possible — from any lurking danger. Small sanctuaries are built in the inconspicuous space underneath an eave, the curve in a gutter's downspout, or in between the joining of two sturdy tree branches, with some species using lichen for camouflage. It's protection against the harsh elements of nature's uncertainties.

We watch and wait, as does the protective mother, who doesn't hesitate — not for a single moment — to hone in on any potentially-destructive prey, willing to destroy any attempts to reach the primitive, yet meticulously-designed shelter. We continue to watch and wait for treasures that will gift to us sweet songs and flights of fancy, and moments of rest. And in the waiting, we yearn for the quick development of their growth, in order to wrench from them a habitat that no longer serves its purpose, save for our own desire to possess that which we had nothing to do with building. We sit and watch it with admiration and envy, knowing that they are chuckling between those sweet notes of song at our own resistance to relinquish a control that we never had.

We marvel at the indestructible nature of their architectural pursuits. We marvel at the unflinching nature of their protective instincts as we fail at our own. And we marvel at the natural mystery that they keep under lock and key, as we try in vain to pick it like a jewel thief in the night, threatening their very existence while trying oh so desperately to hold on to our own.

It's the smallest pieces of discarded twigs and branches that seem to build the strongest, most comfortable bedding to hatch the fledglings. And yet, they are the most difficult to gather, for they are seldom in plain view, instead seeking their own shelter underneath a larger fallen branch. And yet, I am undeterred in my attempts.

TAUT STRINGS BIND AND TIE,
UNTIL THE PUPPETEER DIES.

HANDWRITTEN LETTERS

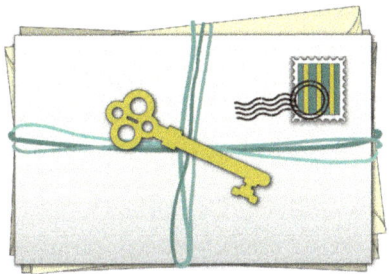

The slant of letters on a heavy pulp piece of parchment paper sets the tone, not unlike a stage in a dramatic production on Broadway: the seductive backdrop in all its stark presentation, the layering upon layering of accoutrements— tables and chairs, artwork, collected treasures, and lighting. Each addition increasing in scale and importance or insignificance, yet essential to the overall presentation and completion of the performance.

Each letter of each word connected and yet completely separate. Meaningless without the connection, except to their own individual, independent nature. And yet knowing with complete conviction that they were created to be joined, to produce meaning. The curves and the slants, the horizontal and vertical symmetry, the dots, the full and half circles, and the ovals and the triangles suggest a bit of arithmetical interference, a mingling of disciplines. The intersections . . . ahhh, the alluring intersections. And all of that in just the stylized representation of the alphabet, capitalization from A to Z, lower case a to z: remembrances of perfectly-aligned wooden desk chairs and certain teachers with an even more certain wooden pointer and sing-song rhyme. And the rapid journey to cursive writing promises epistolary masterpieces that unfurl — promised or not — heartache and magnificence, life cycle announcements, and the very juiciest fencing gossip.

The appearance of a handwritten letter in a nondescript mailbox brings a rush of adrenaline, tossing like a set of jacks the calls for payment to utilities and cable and gasoline and dry cleaning. The copper kettle is filled and brought to a shrill whistle; as the flap is delicately released, and the parchment even more delicately revealed. We take our first sip from our favorite mug and enjoy chamomile tea, settling back in our worn, slipcovered, faded floral print upholstered chair to read and read and read, stopping at times to cry or laugh or envy.

And yet, until it's addressed it cannot begin the journey. The writing is just the start. The salutation is perhaps, in some cases, a hesitancy — and yet, it is written. Sometimes mailed, sometimes taking up long-term residency in a slender slot of a desk, waiting for an indeterminate period of time. And sometimes — most often — it is signed. And upon arrival, it is either received warmly and treasured among beribboned others, or maybe shredded and forgotten. And in the closing, emotions swell; then the folding, either in half or in thirds begins the final process, as it is slid inside the awaiting envelope. But it is in the moistening of the inside of the envelope's flap and the immediacy of sealing and the pressing of the flap firmly against the outside of the envelope that brings a more certain close. And yet, the final phase of addressing the front of the envelope and selecting the perfect stamp — perhaps a renowned literary or sports figure, a flower, animal, or object — still doesn't yet complete the process. The final journey does not begin until it's tossed with precision and delicacy into the open mouth of the mailbox; it's on its way, always uncertain of its arrival and reception.

TAUT STRINGS BIND AND TIE,
UNTIL THE PUPPETEER DIES.

PHOTOGRAPHS

The viewfinder creates a vertigo effect — hypnotic. And without our even realizing it, we are reminded of Kim Novak's character in Hitchcock's *Vertigo*, when we find ourselves lost in the web of a silky, shimmering chignon; not even the sound of the camera's shutter awakens us from our stupor. It's both unnerving and inviting. It's also sought after and repeated, as unsettling as it may be. And it's the anticipation of an image that surfaces that suggests something greater, and yet the surface presents what is, rather than what we wish. But in our anticipation of the unveiling, something greater, deeper than what truly is captivates us — time and time again.

Socrates said, "Be the person you pretend to be," but we challenge even his directive perhaps with more vehemence than ever before, in a society rife with self. And disturbingly, we find not much fault with that approach, until we suddenly do: a moment that when revealed causes us to seek shelter from the reality of it all in a web of our own construction.

Photographs surface from long ago of relatives who, as incredulous as it might sound, were very much like we are today in presenting their best selves. Smiling for the camera at birthday celebrations, wearing cone-shaped paper party hats, and unwinding paper noisemakers. Arm in arm they grin with a certain uncertain conviction emerging from the center aisle of a church after a wedding ceremony, the cascade of blooming white roses and calla lilies, ferns, and billowing white satin ribbons. Children splash in inflated backyard pools, giggles ricocheting off scorched summer surfaces.

Christmas trees are adorned with fragile, multicolored ornaments, and tinsel drips from the tips of Fraser fir branches like silver honey, lights twinkling in the darkened night. Vacation snapshots preserve memories of the Grand Canyon, the Appalachian Mountains, the monuments of Washington, D. C., and the white sands of southern beaches. The roars from the midway edge closer, and the cacophony of sounds bounce off the mid-town cement skyscrapers in Manhattan, as travelers scurry for discounted theater tickets and stand in line for a lukewarm hot dog just to stake their claim to having eaten a lukewarm hot dog on a crowded street corner in New York City.

Easter bonnets and shiny black patent leather Mary Janes adorn children waiting for the Easter Bunny, and shrill cries echo faintly from bundled and cranky youngsters on the lap of Santa Claus at the department store. Newborn babies tucked tight inside their masterfully-executed cocoon-like wrappings, yearning to return from whence they came. The elderly surrounded by an umbrella of loving, loyal, yet potentially blistering, greedy relatives, as if to say, "All is well."

And it's in the looking closely and the observation of the details that is most revealing, most telling. And with the unveiling of sheer, unadulterated truth, we come to know them and ourselves fully, while doing everything in our power to keep the revelation in the shadows. But Socrates has a way of infiltrating that closely-held protection. He's run the gauntlet before, and he'll keep running it as long as the camera's shutter awakens us in an abrupt, yet totally unexpected way, reminding us over and over again to be the person we pretend to be.

TAUT STRINGS BIND AND TIE,
UNTIL THE PUPPETEER DIES.

SEASHELLS

Can you hear it? Listen. It's there, but you need to listen. *Really* listen. Can you do that? I know. You think it's a myth, and maybe it is. You think listening is for children, and you'd be right. But as we're told, it's the children who will lead us. It's true. You know it's true. So take a deep breath and listen. *Really* listen. You'll hear what you're longing to hear.

It's a gathering, a mix: a colorful gathering of a mixture of textures, the fragrance of the waters of the oceans, variances in size and form, a mingling of the different, the unique. And yet, it is also a mingling of the same, without resistance or intolerance. And yet each one brings to the table, in all its uniqueness, a true acceptance of the others' qualities and endurance, hidden treasures and vulnerabilities.

Alpha and Omega. Yin and yang. Beginning and end. Similar and not. Connected yet separate. Dependent yet independent. Defined hues and pearl-like opalescence. Sturdy and delicate. And yet, discordance and harmony, exist side by side, without travail among an estimated 100,000 species worldwide. In complete acceptance, opposites in union. Creating beauty, interest, harmony.

Created by an animal that lives in the sea and part of the body of that animal, yet completely distinct. In the scientific world, it is identified by terms such as exoskeleton, invertebrate, calcium carbonate or chitin, mollusks and barnacles and brachiopods and cephalopods. And we are left with the universality of the collective, while celebrating the uniqueness of each individual seashell.

Seashells have played a part in religion and spirituality. The sand dollar and cowries, as symbols of female fertility. They have been used as musical wind instruments, most commonly in the form of conch trumpets. And seashell ornamentation in the form of necklaces and pendants, earrings and brooches and rings, and hair combs and belt buckles has been practiced since prehistoric times. Crafts, architectural decoration, art, and even poultry feeds all claim the resiliency and use of the seashell, the collaboration of nonresistance in service.

Imagine the possibilities. Imagine the results. Imagine the collective world. Are you listening?

TAUT STRINGS BIND AND TIE,
UNTIL THE PUPPETEER DIES.

HATS

The hats we wear, both figuratively and literally, either lighten our travels or increase the weight of our steps, whether chosen or imparted unwillingly but necessarily. This "shaped covering for the head" comes in many forms: ascot cap, beanie, beret, biretta, bonnet (sun or baby), bowler, cloche, dunce, Gatsby, mitre, mortarboard, Santa, sombrero, top, Tyrolean, zucchetto. And then there's the millinery accoutrements: fancy trims and buttons and bows, hatpins and feathers, jewel-encrusted ornamental embellishments. Royalty and hobo alike wear them. Hat: a simple, three-letter word, carrying with it the weight of the world—or the trivialities of the foolish.

There are hat idioms with layer upon layer of meaning, implied or otherwise: "pass the hat," "toss one's hat in the ring," "at the drop of a hat," and "old hat." Others signify the collection of money among those with and without; the announcement of one's intention to compete against others for something, especially in a political race; without delay or good reason; uninteresting, predictable, commonplace; meaningless or not.

Legend reports that St. Clement, the patron saint of felt, accidentally invented the material when he and St. Christopher escaped from persecution by the Romans. Another legend suggests that felt was discovered by a frustrated Persian shepherd. Still another claims that the material was discovered when the animals on Noah's ark shed their fleece and trampled it underfoot. But legends are just that, legends. In truth the material existed before Christianity was widespread. As with most everything, the beginnings are far-reaching—yet we gleefully announce, over and over, that we were the ones to create and introduce it, at least until the blinding truth is uncovered, with all its glorious imperfections.

Felt is made by matting, condensing, and pressing fibers together. As protection from the harsh elements of wind and rain, snow and sun, the hat covers the head and offers a shield against uninvited intrusions that have the power to injure, damage, harm, or impair: to cause us to suffer. It contracts and expands, prompting adjustment, compromise, flexibility. And as it remembers the shape of the crown, it acts too as a reminder of what has gone before, a familiar companion on a day's journey of uncertainty.

Its many forms are donned and removed, reassessed and experimented with. Baby bonnets, Scout beanies, mortarboards may be commonplace for most, with others trying on for comfort bowlers and cloches, with the zucchetto reserved for the chosen. Brocades and jewels are reserved for the foolish, ornamented elite. And we each, "pass the hat," empty or not, with only the very foolish or the very wise "tossing their hat into the ring." And "at the drop of a hat," well . . . Anything is possible, and either fortunate or not. And "old hat" is a possibility that none of us wants to entertain, yet we each know it's apparent sooner or later, praying for the first to avoid the latter. But we wear them anyway—at times, more than one—until we toss them on the seat of a vacant chair or the hook of a coat rack, steady to hit the mark.

TAUT STRINGS BIND AND TIE,
UNTIL THE PUPPETEER DIES.

28

ABOUT THE AUTHOR

KATHLEEN M. JACOBS is the author of *Honeysuckle Holiday*, a YA-novel set in the south in the 1960s, *Marble Town*, a MG-novel about a young boy coming to terms with the unexpected death of his mother, and *Collected Curiosities: Poems, Essays, & Opinions*. Her first children's book, *Please Close It!*, illustrated by Ashley Teets was released in 2018 and took Honorable Mention at the San Francisco, Paris, and New York Book Festivals. She lives in West Virginia (and sometimes in New York City) with her husband, John. Visit her website at www.kathleenmjacobs.com and on Twitter: @KathleenMJacobs, as well as FB: Kathleen M. Jacobs, Author.

www.ingramcontent.com/pod-product-compliance
Lightning Source LLC
Chambersburg PA
CBHW042146170626
46815CB00006BA/331